Summer at *Izzie's*

Written by *Will Green*

P.O. Box 483
Strawberry Point, Iowa 52076
Phone: 563 933 6704
Additional information is available at
www.greenstreetgifts.com

Illustrated by *David R. Prehm*

Illustrations by David R. Prehm

ISBN: 1450540988
ISBN-13: 9781450540988

Contents

This book is dedicated to my parents, Charles and Donna, who blessed our family by spending many hours on the farm with Menerva and Fred Green. Menerva and Fred were the inspiration for this fictional glimpse of daily life on a small Iowa farm in the mid twentieth century. Their demonstration of hard work, kindness, and caring continue to impact those who knew them.

Chapter 1

Izzie's

    My best friend Nancy moved at the end of the school year. Summer would be different without Nancy to chum around with. It wouldn't be near as much fun running into Mr. Verbut's grocery store to get an ice cream sandwich or a bag of candy, or going to get a soda at Hayford's drugstore. I would have to be satisfied with writing an occasional letter to Nancy and hope that she would write back. I guess I would just spend more of my summer helping Izzie on the farm.

    Izzie's farm was nearly halfway between the small towns of Lamont and Aurora. The Chicago Great Western Railway sliced through the small eighty-acre farm, making it a relatively short walk from either town if you walked along the railway. If I rode my bike, it was at least a mile longer than walking the rails. Either way could be an adventure.

    Most days I rode my bike north out of town on the blacktop and then west down a gravel road. This route took me past the Lang and Gerdeman farms and then by the old Lockwood place. When I passed the Lockwood's, two of their three dogs would nearly always bark, race alongside me, and nip at my feet no matter how fast I peddled. If I were in luck, Mr. Lockwood would be out tending to his cattle and would call the dogs off.

This morning I was in luck. Mr. Lockwood was herding his cows out to the pasture as I peddled past. His dogs were helping with the herding, so they paid little attention to me. As I reached the curve where the gravel road once again swung north, I slowed my bike and struck out on an old abandoned dirt road that went directly to the northeast corner of Izzie's farm. The trail of the road was quite faint; it was once used by horses and wagons heading westward, and Mr. Lockwood only used it occasionally. The trail led up a small, sandy knoll then dipped into a shallow marshy area where a small creek flowed. Even though it was June, it was quite dry. I managed to coast right to the creek's edge before jumping off and pushing the bike through the water. A few marsh marigolds and the very last of the shooting stars were scattered about as I walked the bike up the old road to the top of Sand Hill. On this side of the creek there was only a single path. I wanted to stop and pick some of the flowers for Izzie, but my hands were full, and I had no pockets suitable for carrying flowers.

As I reached Izzie's fence, I stopped to catch my breath and looked around. The view from Izzie's portion of Sand Hill was always breathtaking. You could see both Lamont and Aurora, as well as numerous farms scattered about the countryside. It was peaceful here. Only the wind blowing through an old gnarled cottonwood tree, the occasional quack of a duck from the marsh, and the song of the meadow lark broke the serenity.

I squeezed my bike between two fence posts that marked the boundary between the Recker farm and Izzie's. It was all downhill from here. I coasted most of the way, and the cattle lane I followed led me behind the barn to a gate, and then into Izzie's yard.

After maneuvering my bike through the barnyard gate and locking it behind me, I could see that Izzie had clothes on the line blowing in the warm breeze. Izzie was stooped over picking the first of the June strawberries. She had her apron on, and the pockets were bulging with strawberries. Izzie always whistled while she worked, and I could hear her cheerful song as I approached.

I began to whistle too. I didn't want to startle Izzie. Smokey, Izzie's dog, perked his ears and let out a mighty bark alerting Izzie. Apparently Smokey didn't want Izzie to be startled either. Izzie turned my way almost as if she were expecting me. She brushed her silver-streaked auburn hair from her face. Her green eyes sparkled when she saw me.

"Well, how was the bike ride this morning, Julie?" Before I could answer, Izzie had her arm around me and gave me a kiss on the forehead. She often hugged me, but the strawberries in her apron would have gotten squished if she'd hugged me today.

"Looks like you got your feet a little wet crossing the creek," commented Izzie.

"Yes, I couldn't jump across and pull the bike along at the same time," I replied smiling.

"I see," Izzie replied, nodding.

Izzie and I headed for her house. It was a typical white, small, two-story farmhouse. Quaint. A windbreak of white pines, willows, and honeysuckle bushes sheltered the home from winter's frigid winds and summer's scorching afternoon sun. We passed by the rhubarb patch, the asparagus bed, and several flower gardens. One garden contained peonies, iris, and spent tulips. Another had phlox, pansies, daisies, and other flowers that I didn't recognize. I wouldn't have recognized any of them if it hadn't been for Izzie. Hollyhocks surrounded the back porch and a miniature rose climbed a small trellis between the porch and the cellar doors. These were the cellar doors that had to be repaired years ago when Izzie's husband, Fred, accidentally drove the car up on them. That was when Fred was young and was just learning to drive a Model T. Of course, Izzie didn't talk about that when Fred was home.

When we reached the porch steps, Izzie instructed me to leave my shoes on the steps and let the sunshine dry them. She also told Smokey to go lay under the tree.

When Izzie opened the back door, the smell of freshly baked cookies escaped outside and was scattered about by the warm summer breeze. It was a tradition that when I visited, we would always start our day together by having a cookie or two and something to drink. I would always choose fresh *farm* milk to drink and Izzie would usually choose tea, which she brewed on her new electric stove.

Electricity was rather new to Izzie and Fred. They were the very last in their neighborhood to get *hooked up*. Many of the neighbors had electricity ten to fifteen years earlier. Electricity was new enough to Izzie that she still had her old wood-burning cook stove in place on the south side of her kitchen. She liked to use both stoves— the cook stove on cool mornings to make pancakes and the electric stove in the afternoons for canning or baking. Both Izzie and Fred were kind of straddling the old and the new.

Despite having electricity, there were still things on Izzie's farm that were old fashioned. Izzie had to pump water by hand from the well to drink and to water the animals. She also had a cistern that caught rainwater. This, too, had a hand pump and was used for washing clothes, washing hands, and other household tasks. They still had two horses, Jerry and Ginger, which Fred used for light farm chores like hauling manure or dragging the fields before planting. Most of their heavy work like plowing and disking was taken over by a two-cylinder John Deere tractor.

Izzie and Fred had a radio but no TV. They had lights and lamps but no fans. They had a car, but only Fred could drive. They had cows to milk but no milking machine. They had a well with water but no pipe to the house to provide running water; that meant they had an outhouse instead of a bathroom. So no matter what the weather, night or day, you had to run outside and down the stone path to the outhouse to go to the bathroom. It also meant that the large wash-tub hanging on the back porch was not just used for laundry—it did double duty as a bathtub. A bathroom is one thing that Izzie wished for.

After our cookie break, Izzie and I headed back outside into the warm sunshine. My shoes were still damp, but I knew they would soon dry. I wondered what we would do today. As we stepped onto the garden path, Jerry and Ginger whinnied. They were standing near the livestock water tank.

"Well, I guess we better pump some water into the stock tank for the horses. They didn't go out with the cows to the pasture this morning because Fred is going to use them this afternoon to haul some rocks to the creek."

Fred had taken a job with the railroad after his family had grown and left home. He worked maintaining and repairing the rails. He was a short powerful man, and despite being in his sixties, had biceps like softballs and could lift two feed bags over his head with relative ease. He could always be seen wearing a pair of bib overalls with his watch in one bib pocket and a bulging billfold in the other. He kept his bald head covered by one type of hat or another, but even with the hat, his bulbous nose took much punishment from the summer sun. He was a man, generally, of few words. However, when he spoke, you were expected to listen. People might get the impression that he was kind of gruff and opinionated mainly because he was…at times. But no matter what your impression of Fred, you knew he had good taste—after all, he had chosen Izzie to be his bride.

After we pumped enough water to fill the livestock tank, we threw several ears of corn to the six sows and their piglets that were penned near the corncrib. We also pumped a couple of buckets of water for the sows and dumped it in a wooden trough that lay in the muddy pen. The piglets were still nursing, so it was important to give the sows as much water as they would drink.

We walked between the hog house and the corncrib toward the garden, which was near Izzie's small chicken house. A hen cackled, signaling that she had just laid an egg. This was a reminder to gather the eggs before one was pecked or stepped on and broken. We gathered eight eggs, which according to Izzie wasn't bad for twelve old laying hens.

I walked the small egg basket over to the back porch and set it inside, and then returned to Izzie's side at the garden.

"Well, Julie Belle, we've got some serious weeding to do in this garden before lunch," Izzie said.

Izzie and I stooped, squatted, and crawled through each row of sweet corn, green beans, peas, potatoes, onions, lettuce, cabbage, beets, cucumbers, and squash, pulling every weed that dared grow. Even after Izzie's family was raised, she continued to carry on as always. Growing the same things in the same quantities that she always did, but now she canned and preserved less and gave away more.

Izzie and I heard Lamont's noon whistle. We had just one short row to go, so we plucked the last of the weeds and headed toward the house for lunch. We made a short detour by the well to get a cool drink and wash our hands. There was always a cup hanging from the windmill and a bar of soap under a tin can. The windmill itself wasn't working. The gearbox had to be repaired, and Izzie and Fred were too old to make the repairs themselves, so until some courageous soul climbed up there to make the repair, the blades only spun in the breeze. If the windmill were repaired, the wind would do much of the water pumping that was now done by hand.

After our lunch of ham sandwiches, potato salad, green beans, milk, and more homemade cookies, Izzie and I were ready for the afternoon. We gathered the laundry from the line first. Izzie then put me to work folding clothes, while she ironed shirts, bib overalls, aprons, housedresses, handkerchiefs, and a tablecloth. There wasn't really that much for me to do because Izzie ironed almost everything except underwear and socks.

When the laundry was done, Izzie and I went into her sewing room, which had been the pantry at one time. Izzie loved to sew. After electricity was installed Fred bought Izzie a Singer electric sewing machine. Now Izzie had two Singers—one electric and one pedal powered. She was working on a dress for one of her granddaughters. It was a summer dress, and the material was white with pastel stripes. The dress was the same size as I wore, so I was her model. I wore the dress while Izzie pinned the hem. After the hem was finished, which didn't take long, it was time to get the mail.

The mail came at about three o'clock. Walter, the mailman, was pretty punctual. There were times, however, when Mr. Griffin or one of Izzie's other neighbors might stop him and visit about the crops, grain prices, or the weather. Today the flag was down on the mailbox, which meant that Walter had been there and had taken a letter written by Izzie and perhaps left her something. As we walked down the long driveway, Smokey loped ahead hoping to surprise a rabbit or a pheasant. Izzie whistled as we walked, and I admired all the wild strawberry blossoms and wild roses in the ditch. I could hardly wait until the wild strawberries would be ripe. They were much sweeter than the tame variety that Izzie had in her garden and were best suited for grazing, as Izzie would say. Which meant eating them on our trips to and from the mailbox.

A Sears and Roebuck catalog came in the mail along with a letter from the Martins, who were relatives of Izzie and Fred. I carried the catalog back to the house while Izzie read the letter to me. It sounded as though all was well with the Martins, who lived a half a world away on a farm in Grange-over-Sands, England. When we reached the yard, Izzie and I sat in the shade of the pines and looked through the new catalog. Time flew by, but there was one more thing I wanted to do before I left for home.

"Isn't it time to go get the cows?" I asked.

"I believe it is," Izzie replied, looking at the sky because she had no watch on.

Izzie always got the cows up from the pasture, put them in the barn, and fed them before Fred got home. This saved him time, and Izzie could make supper while he milked. The six Jersey cows were in the south pasture. Izzie had herded them there in the morning after she milked them. She always did the morning milking because Fred had to be on the job at daybreak. She often remarked how the electric lights in the barn made her job a lot easier but that a milking machine would be even better. Of course, with six cows, a milking machine would hardly be practical.

As Izzie and I strolled hand- in- hand down the cow lane to the south pasture, she whistled, and I watched and listened for the train. At that time there was no train to be seen or heard. The cows were across the railroad tracks from the barn. All six of them were near the gate when we reached the top of the railway grade, chewing their cuds and swishing flies with their tails. They appeared to be a contented lot. It wouldn't be much of a trick today to get the cows across the track and headed toward the barn. Their bellies were full, and their udders were heavy with milk. I went across and opened the gate, and Izzie called the cows across.

"Come, Bossie. Come, Boss," she said.

Over the tracks the cows trudged, past Izzie and up the lane toward the barn.

"That was easy," I told Izzie.

Izzie closed the gate behind us and remarked, "It's always easy when there's lots of grass to eat. But when the weather gets dry, and the pasture gets short in August, those six can be a handful. They'll want to wander down the railroad ditch beside the tracks and graze where the grass is greener. That's when we will have to take them by the halter and lead them across one by one."

In the distance a train tooted its whistle. Ole' number nine was passing through Aurora and headed our way. It blew its whistle at each road crossing. It wasn't long, and it was only a mile away at the crossing near the Gates' farm. Izzie stopped.

"Let's wait and see if George is driving the train today."

George was Fred's brother who was an engineer and often passed this way on his route to Chicago. Fred, George, and their sister, Gladys, were raised on Izzie's farm. When George and Gladys left to start their lives elsewhere, Fred stayed on the farm and helped his parents work the land until they passed away.

The train sounded its whistle as it passed us by. Smoke belched from the locomotive's stack. The steel wheels screeched against the steel rails and groaned under the weight of the engine and the many coal and grain cars it pulled. The engineer waved. Izzie and I waved back. It wasn't George at the controls but some other friendly engineer. The train's clickety-clack and screeching faded as it motored eastward. It would soon sound its whistle again when it neared the first crossing at Lamont.

The cows reached the barn long before Izzie and me. We each chewed on some orchard grass, and Izzie showed me how to make a screeching noise by holding a blade of grass between your thumbs and blowing on it. I wasn't very successful, but Izzie had it mastered. I preferred her whistling, however.

As we strolled toward the barnyard, Izzie and I visited and whistled.

"Julie, I sure wish I had a bathroom like you have in your house in town. A nice soak in the tub would sure feel good after the work is done. Of course, having an inside toilet would be wonderful too. That walk to the outhouse can be a long one when you get to be my age."

"I wish I had a gas-powered lawn mower like a lot of folks do. A TV would be nice and a telephone, too. I wish someday to learn to drive a car. Wish, wish, wish." She paused briefly, gazed dreamily across the fields, and then continued. "The good part about wishing is that it doesn't cost anything. What do you wish for, Julie?"

"I wish I could stay awhile longer. I love spending time here with you," I answered.

"I wish you could too, Julie Belle. But you know, I had one wish come true today. That wish was that you would come and spend the day with me."

I smiled and gave Izzie a hug. It was time to go.

"You better run along before it gets any later. We don't want your mom to worry."

I ran to get my bike, and let myself through the gate behind the barn. As I passed, Izzie opened the barn door to let the cows in. She waved, and I did the same. I ran the bike up Sand Hill, squeezed the bike between the posts, coasted down the rough path to the creek, splashed the bike and me through the water, and then walked the bike to the top of the last knoll. Then I rode my bike as fast as my legs would peddle. Past the Lockwood farm and their pesky dogs all the way home.

Chapter 2 *Back Home*

As I rode up our drive on Oak Street, I could see that my brothers were home. There were three bikes leaning haphazardly by the back steps. Before I opened the door, I could hear the radio blaring. All three boys were seated around our kitchen table, heads in their hands, listening intently to a ball game. It was the ninth inning and the Cubs were behind the Cardinals four to three. I think the whole neighborhood could have heard the announcer when the radio wasn't crackling and popping with static. There must have been a thunderstorm between WGN's radio tower in Chicago and our place. I was kind of glad Ernie Banks flew out to the centerfielder for the last out because that static was really annoying after being at a place as peaceful as Izzie's farm.

Two of my brothers, Bill and Ron, were older than me. They were close in age—only fifteen months separated them. Because they were so close, they did almost everything together. It was rare to see one without the other either playing ball or helping some of the farmers in the area pick up rocks, pull weeds, or bale hay. They often helped Fred and Izzie. Dad would even help at Izzie's in the evenings if he got home from the factory at a reasonable hour. Oh, and of course there was my younger brother Wally who tagged Bill and Ron around. He seemed like he was forever at an awkward stage. When he wasn't running, stumbling, or falling, he was riding his bike, zigzagging his way around the streets of Lamont with his pants rolled up a cuff or two and his shoelaces untied. There were many days when those shoelaces either got tangled in his bike chain or tripped him while he was running. I was glad that Bill and Ron had looked after him today.

I had just poured myself a glass of water, when I heard a car door in the drive. Mom was home! Now that the boys and I could look after ourselves (or at least each other), Mom had decided to go back to college to get her teaching degree. She was taking summer classes at the university about twenty-five miles from our home. Since Dad drove the car to work every day, Mom was fortunate to be able to ride with Wanda Carpenter who lived near town. She was much younger than Mom, just out of high school, and was going to school to be a teacher also.

"Hi, Mom!" I shrieked excitedly as she entered the kitchen door. "Izzie and I sure got a lot done on the farm today!" Then before Mom even set her books down I explained in vivid detail everything that Izzie and I had done that day.

"Wow!" Mom exclaimed. "What will Izzie do tomorrow if you got all those things done today?" She smiled.

"Well, probably just about the same things we did today. I don't think she ever gets caught up. That's why I like to go out there," I answered. "And, of course, for the cookies!"

"Oh, of course, the cookies!" Mom smiled. "It seems to me that everything Izzie cooks or bakes is good. She's a terrific cook," Mom added as she set her books on the kitchen table. "Julie, why don't you and I try to make something almost as good as Izzie's?" She paused. "How about shepherd's pie?"

"That doesn't sound like something Izzie would make," I commented, raising my eyebrows and smiling a little.

"It may not be as good as something Izzie would make, but it'll fill your growling stomach and your brothers' hollow legs," Mom said as she smiled and winked at me. We both grinned.

Dad rolled into the drive about six o'clock. Twenty minutes later, we were all at the table, prayer said, and gobbling down our food between pieces of conversation. Mom talked about her class, Dad talked about work, I talked about my day at Izzie's, Bill and Ron talked about their ball game with Dundee, and Wally…well, he just ate.

Chapter 3 *Return Trip to Izzie's*

The static that interfered with the radio must have been an omen. We had rain and thunderstorms for the next few days. Staying at home was pleasant for the most part. There were no ball games to play, no hay to make, and it was too far to go to Izzie's in the rain. My brothers and I read, played board games, card games, and snacked. There was, however, occasional arguing, hollering, laughing, and bickering amongst us, and an entertaining wrestling match erupted between Bill and Ron. In between games and antics I did manage to get a letter written to my friend Nancy. As for Wally… he played, laughed, practiced tying double knots in his shoelaces, and ate a lot.

On Thursday, July 2, the weather cleared. A brisk northwest breeze blew wispy clouds across the blue sky. I couldn't wait to get back to Izzie's to see what there was to do. I took my usual route down the gravel road past Lockwood's (and their dogs), down the old abandoned road, and to the creek. Mom had cautioned me about crossing the creek when the water was high. Today the creek was swollen. The creek was twice as wide as normal. Instead of being three feet from bank to bank, it was six feet across. I could see the bottom, though, and it didn't look dangerous. I decided it would be best to leave my bike behind in the grass. I took off my shoes, tied the shoelaces together and threw them over my shoulder. I rolled my pant legs up to my knees and forded the creek. Unfortunately, the creek was higher than I thought and the water soaked my pants clear to the bottom of my pockets. I teetered a little in the current, hoping not to fall and get a complete soaking. I carefully made my next step and was relieved to feel bedrock and shallower water. I quickly scampered up the other side of the creek and was happy to have only suffered two wet pant legs and a blow to my dignity.

The wind quickly began to dry my jeans as I walked up Sand Hill and past the gnarly cottonwood tree. As I squeezed between the posts and on to Izzie's land, I startled a rooster pheasant, and he cackled as he flew across Fred's corn, which was now about knee high. As I walked down the lane toward Izzie's barn, I noticed that Fred had planted some melons in a little spot the corn planter had missed. This melon patch was Fred's garden. He never wanted Izzie to waste her good garden space on melons, which in Iowa were not always productive. But Fred's success with melons on Sand Hill was gaining him somewhat of a reputation—such a reputation that the neighbor boys had been known to *borrow* a few during the dark warm nights in August. *Borrow*, in this case, was Izzie's nice way of saying stealing. Izzie had a way of overlooking imperfections and flaws and only seeing the good in things and in others. It was a gift— a gift that rubbed off on you if you were around Izzie for very long. Fred, however, just sputtered and called it plain old stealing.

As I continued to descend Sand Hill, I could see Izzie leading Jerry and Ginger away from the barn. They were pulling a stone boat, which looked like a crude toboggan, with three cans of milk loaded on it. Izzie didn't usually do much with the horses and the machinery. That was men's work, as Fred would say. Izzie was wearing her work jeans, a light jacket, and her knee boots; not her usual attire. She nearly always wore one of her everyday housedresses inside and out. Her slight frame looked even smaller while she worked with the horses.

Smokey sounded the alarm, and Izzie stopped the horses. I ran to Izzie's side, and she gave me a hug.

"I wondered if you would be over today. I was kind of worried that the creek would be too swift for you to cross," Izzie said as she surveyed my clothing. "From the looks of your jeans, the creek must have been a little high," she commented.

"Yes. It was kind of high. But I could see the bottom, and the current wasn't too strong. I left my bike on the other side. I didn't want to risk having it tip over in the water and taking me with it," I said.

"Well, at least you kept your shoes dry, and it looks like your jeans will soon be dry with this breeze blowing." The horses pulled impatiently at the reins in Izzie's hands. "Julie, go over to the porch and sit in the sun while I take this milk down the driveway to the road. It's too muddy for the milkman to bring the truck up into the yard. I'll be back shortly. Take Smokey with you. He'll be good company," Izzie directed.

As Smokey and I headed toward the sunny side of the porch, I watched Izzie drive Jerry and Ginger down the muddy driveway to leave the stone boat and milk near the mailbox for the milkman. It wasn't long before Izzie returned and placed Jerry and Ginger in the barnyard with the cows. She stopped by the well and pumped some water into the livestock tank before she walked to the porch.

"Well, Julie Belle, let me get these muddy boots off, and I'll run inside and get each of us a couple of cookies and milk, and we can eat them out here in the sunshine."

Izzie soon returned with the cookies and milk.

"I bet you were you surprised to see me working with the horses this morning."

Izzie explained that Fred had to work overnight near Stanley. The rain the last few days caused a washout, and he and the crew had to get some ties and track replaced before the morning train got there from Chicago.

After swallowing a mouthful of chocolate chip cookie I replied. "I was surprised—and even more surprised that you were wearing jeans and those boots."

Izzie smiled and pulled me close to her. "Well, honey, I've been known to surprise a few people in my day, and my days aren't over yet."

Izzie reached into her jacket pocket. "Don't tell anyone this, but I often carry this with me around the farm when I'm here alone. I used to carry it more before we got Smokey." Izzie carefully turned her calloused hand over and showed me what she had. I gasped. It was a gun! It was the smallest gun I'd ever seen. A pistol! I'd never seen a real pistol before. I had often seen the shotguns and rifles that my dad and brothers used to hunt pheasants and rabbits. Even Izzie's Fred had a couple of guns. But never had I seen a gun like this. Izzie with a gun? It was like seeing an angel with a pitchfork!

Izzie must have sensed my disbelief. She put her hand on my shoulder. "Julie, are you alright?"

"I think so," I stammered. "I'm just surprised."

"See, Julie, I told you I could surprise people."

"Surprise people! You could scare the devil right out of someone with that thing!" I exclaimed.

Izzie went on to explain that hobos often frequented the rail lines. They were mostly looking for food when they came to your door, but there could be a bad one now and then, and Fred just wanted her to have the gun for safety.

Izzie and I went to work after our cookie break. We herded the cows and horses across the tracks to the south pasture and spent the remainder of the morning picking strawberries. Izzie had a bumper crop of strawberries. We picked twelve quart baskets of berries—more than you could eat!

After our lunch of leftovers, Izzie and I made strawberry preserves, which was no small task. We had to haul water from the pump to wash the berries, take the stems off, mash them, mix them with lots of sugar and fruit pectin, and cook them until they boiled. We then ladled them into jam jars with the hope that as the jam cooled, the zinc lids on top would seal. If they sealed properly, they could be stored at room temperature until they were needed, which might be some wintery January morning.

I looked up as Izzie's clock chimed once. It was already half past three.

"Izzie, I better get back to town."

"Oh my, is it that late already?" Izzie sighed and wiped her forehead. "Don't worry, Julie, I'll finish cleaning this up later. I'll go out with you, and then bring the cows and horses up from the south pasture. Hopefully, Fred will be home tonight. Oh, don't forget to remind your parents that they are invited out here on the Fourth."

"Okay, Izzie. I'll tell them."

"And Julie, be careful crossing the creek."

I felt like replying, "And Izzie, don't shoot anyone with that gun." But instead I just giggled inside.

I walked briskly up Sand Hill. I had forgotten all about being invited to Izzie's for the Fourth of July. That would be such fun. Izzie was always in her glory when friends and family filled her house. As I topped the hill near the gnarly cottonwood tree, I caught myself whistling just like Izzie. Down the hill I hiked to the creek, waded across it with my shoes over my shoulder, grabbed my bike, and walked it up the knoll to the gravel road near Lockwood's. As I rode home, I thought of all the things Izzie had yet to do before she would sleep.

Izzie had to bring the horses and cows up from the pasture, put the cows in the barn and feed them, hitch and drive the horses down the lane to bring empty milk cans back to the barn, and then place the horses in the barnyard. She would have to clean up our strawberry mess, cook and serve supper, and then wash the dishes. If Fred didn't come home, she would have to do all of his chores. I felt guilty going back to a nice home in town with not only running water and a bathroom, but also many hands to do the chores. I was beginning to understand Izzie's many wishes. As I sped past Lockwood's pesky dogs, I pledged to go to Izzie's every chance I got. I smiled as I thought of Izzie and her gun. Izzie the whistling gunslinger—she'd make a great character in a movie.

Chapter 4 *Preparations*

I awoke to the smell of pancakes cooking and bacon frying. I lay in bed listening to banging cupboard doors, clanging dishes, and rattling silverware. I looked toward my bedroom window and could see a sliver of sunshine trying to brighten the dark room. It was sunny. It would be another great day to be out on the farm helping Izzie. But today was Saturday, and my day would be planned by Mom or Dad. Maybe, Dad would take the boys fishing, and Mom and I could go shopping. Maybe the guys would do yard work and Mom and I could bake. Maybe…

"Hey, wake up you sleepyheads! You're missing the best part of the day! Breakfast is ready," Dad shouted up the stairway.

I heard my brothers' feet hit the floor and decided I'd better do likewise.

While we sat around the kitchen table, mowing down pancakes and bacon there wasn't much conversation. Bill, Ron, and Wally were eating like it would be their last meal. Mom and Dad were guzzling coffee, and I ate and thought about Izzie and her farm.

"When you kids get finished with breakfast, get dressed in your everyday clothes. We're going out to Izzie's to help her get ready for tomorrow," Mom announced.

I wasn't the only one in our family who got excited about going to Izzie's. My brothers loved to explore every nook and cranny of the old barn and wander about the farm looking at all the animals— domestic and wild. Dad enjoyed it too. He liked helping Fred tinker with the tractor, repairing a piece of equipment, or working with the livestock. Mom enjoyed the tours of Izzie's gardens and helping with the cooking and baking. Of course, I enjoyed it all.

I was so excited to be going to Izzie's that I could hardly contain myself. With the whole family there, we could be a lot of help to both Izzie and Fred.

When we arrived, Izzie had gathered some eggs, and Fred was working on the horse-drawn mower. I could see Izzie's lips pursed— whistling as she carried the basket of eggs to the back porch. We piled out of the car, and Izzie greeted each of us with a hug. Fred soon joined the group. His bib overalls were covered with grease, and he smelled of kerosene.

"What do we get to do today, Izzie?" I asked excitedly before any-one else could speak.

"Well, where shall I begin?" She paused. "We are going to have fresh fried chicken for dinner tomorrow. So, I will need someone to drive over to the Dodge's and pick up the five spring fryers I pur-chased. There are buns to bake and potato salad to make. The pies are already made and can be baked when we do the buns. Someone will also need to get the ice cream freezer from the cellar, because tomorrow we're going to have homemade ice cream to go with our pie." My brothers whooped at the mention of homemade ice cream. "I think we'll be well prepared if we get the chickens butchered and the buns and potato salad made," Izzie concluded.

"I could use a little help later with that gearbox on the windmill, but first I've got to get that old mower oiled, greased, and a few sickle blades replaced," Fred added.

Dad and Wally volunteered to go to the Dodge's to get the chick-ens. Izzie said she'd get the hot water going to scald the chickens. Mom and I agreed to peel the potatoes and get the buns stirred up.

Bill and Ron said they would locate the chicken crate and the old hand-crank ice cream maker.

Off we all went to do our duties. Izzie put water on both the cook stove and the electric stove. I ran to the cellar and brought up enough potatoes to feed an army or so it seemed. Mom sifted the flour for the buns. Fred went back to his mower repair. Dad and Wally went to the Dodge's. Bill and Ron completed their small tasks quickly, and when I last saw them, they had Fred's old fish poles, a bucket of worms, and were walking west on the railroad tracks headed for Hartfield's quarry. "A lot of help they are," I thought.

We had the potatoes peeled, and the dough was rising when we heard the horn from our car. Dad and Wally had returned with the chickens. Izzie went to the back porch door.

"Just carry the chickens out between the corncrib and hog house. It'll be cooler there to do the butchering. I'll bring the knives and the hot water," Izzie hollered.

I'd seen chickens butchered before and knew it was a necessary evil, but I preferred to deal with the chickens after they were butchered. Wally, on the other hand had never seen this process and was anxious to see what it was all about. He soon found out.

Before Izzie carried out the hot water, she gathered up several pans, a washtub, knives, an old tablecloth, and dragged an old wooden table out of the lean-to shed that was attached to the corncrib. She'd been through this process many times. She bustled back to the house and carried a bucket of soapy water to the makeshift butcher shop to wash off the dusty old table. I knew the killing wasn't far off.

I could hear the chickens squawking from my ringside seat at the kitchen window. It wasn't long before Izzie came toward the house with a five-gallon pail to get the scalding hot water. It was good that Izzie retrieved the water because it was getting pretty steamy in the kitchen. I can still remember the beads of perspiration on Mom's brow as she kneaded the dough for the buns.

The squawking grew intense. I looked out the window. A headless chicken jumped, bounced, and danced at Wally's feet. He danced too—trying to get away from the bloody thing. Soon another chicken was jumping at Wally's feet. It was gruesome but kind of humorous. Wally and a chicken dancing—this may have been how the so-called *chicken dance* got its name. Soon it grew silent. The killing was over. Now came the plucking. My view from the kitchen window was obstructed by the corncrib. All I could see now was an occasional feather flying in the summer breeze.

Soon the five fryers were butchered and sitting in cold water beneath the windmill. Izzie returned, whistling of course, washed her hands and face, changed her apron, and was ready to move on to the next task.

After Wally and Dad completed the cleanup, which entailed digging a hole in the field, burying the inedible remains of the chickens, and scrubbing all the tubs, pans, and utensils, it was time for lunch. By now the buns and pies were in the oven, and the potatoes were boiled. We were making progress. Fred had made progress too. He had managed to get the old mower fixed, and after lunch planned to mow down a field of timothy hay. Izzie rang the dinner bell outside the back porch as a signal to Bill and Ron that it was lunchtime.

Soon we were all seated at the picnic table beneath the towering white pines eating another feast prepared by Izzie. It was nothing special, according to Izzie, just hot dogs, pork and beans, hot homemade buns, strawberry jam, homemade apple pie, and fresh farm milk.

After the dishes were done, Izzie, Mom, and I sat at the picnic table, watched the men and just visited. Fred had hitched the mower to Jerry and Ginger and was mowing hay. Dad was at the north end of the field with the grease gun and oilcan, just in case they were needed. My brothers decided to be helpful and pumped water into the livestock water tank. They also threw a scoop of corn to the pigs.

Fred only mowed for an hour or so. He unhitched Jerry and Ginger and placed them in the barnyard. He and Dad were going to attempt to fix the windmill gear box. The windmill wasn't very tall, but tall enough to put the fear in you if you had to climb it. Fred found a rope and gave Dad a bag with some wrenches in it.

"Just climb up the ladder and when you get to the top, tie the rope around your waist for safety," Fred instructed Dad.

"You kids stay back. If he drops something, you could get hurt," He added.

Watching Dad climb the windmill was like watching a trapeze artist in a circus climb to his perch before his act began. Mom couldn't bear to watch, so she and Izzie went into the house to finish the potato salad and cut up the chickens for tomorrow's dinner.

When Dad reached the top, a breeze came up and the blades on the windmill spun quite vigorously. The wind swirled a bit, blowing the rudder one way and then the other.

"I need a board to brace this thing," Dad hollered.

Fred handed my brother, Bill, an old oak board and asked if he would carry the board to the top for Dad. Bill agreed, and he carefully, shakily, inched his way toward the top. After what seemed like an eternity, he handed the board to Dad and he successfully wedged the board so the windmill wouldn't spin or pivot. This allowed him to work more safely.

Dad determined a gear was broken and that a bearing was worn out. New ones would be needed to fix the windmill properly. In order to make the repairs more easily, Dad removed the gearbox and lowered it to Fred using the rope. It would be at least another week or so before the final repair could be made. It also meant another trip up the windmill ladder and more hand pumping.

We didn't stay and help with the milking that night. Bill, Ron, and Wally did bring the cows up from the pasture, though, so Fred or Izzie didn't have to do it. As we drove home, despite being exhausted, everyone chattered about something that happened that day at Izzie's. Dad talked about being at the top of the windmill tower, Mom talked about all the food we'd prepared for the Fourth, Bill talked about how courageous he was climbing "Mt. Windmill," Ron talked about how shaky Bill was while climbing, I talked about peeling potatoes, and Wally talked nonstop about headless, jumping chickens.

Chapter 5 *The Fourth*

July the Fourth was a beautiful sunshiny Sunday. After gulping down our breakfast, dressing for church, and fidgeting through one of Pastor Larson's longest sermons of the year, we headed for Izzie's. I knew how the day would start. Today would be a *little* more relaxing. Of course, Izzie would be bustling around the kitchen wearing her Sunday best, and Fred would have his newest bib overalls on. Fred would have all the outside chores done and be sitting in his easy chair reading the newspaper or the *Farm Journal*. Sunday and holidays were Fred's reading days. There wasn't much time on other days. Izzie would have the leaves placed in the old round oak table and have her best tablecloth and silverware out. She would be putting the last touches on the potato salad, have several pies warming in the oven, and be washing all the dishes dirtied from the preparation.

When we arrived Smokey let out his usual bark or two and then retreated to the shade of the nearest pine tree. On real hot days, okey went under the porch and lay next to the cool rock foundation of Izzie's house.

Izzie stepped outside the back porch, drying her hands on her apron, as we bailed out of the car. She greeted each of us with a hug. Mom then handed Izzie a macaroni salad that she had made long before I bounced out of bed and went into the house to help Izzie with the chicken. Dad went in to visit with Fred about farming or politics. Wally and I ran to Izzie's swing that was attached to a branch that extended from the white pine tree nearest the driveway. Wally and I spent more time twisting the swing round and round and spinning then we did swinging. Bill and Ron found an old catcher's mitt and other baseball equipment in Izzie's woodshed and played catch in the orchard west of the chicken house.

It wasn't long before Izzie's other guests began to arrive. Izzie dropped everything as each carload arrived and greeted them in her customary way with hugs, kisses to the forehead, or pats on the shoulder or head. The first guests to arrive were Bill and Gladys Paulson from Oelwein. Gladys, Fred's sister, and Bill or "William" as Gladys called him was a machinist in the railroad shop. My dad and William had common interests—fishing and ball playing.

Soon Izzie and Fred's sons, Dale and Larry, arrived with their families. Dale and his wife, Kathy, had three boys, and Larry and his wife, Alice, had three boys and Jill, who was a couple years younger than me. It wasn't long before Bill and Ron's simple game of catch turned into a game of work up. Wally soon lost interest in the swing and joined the ball game with the rest of the boys.

Jim, Fred and Izzie's oldest son, his wife, Nancy, and their four girls were the last to arrive. Jim always brought a canned ham for Izzie when he visited. He worked at Rath Packing in Waterloo, Iowa, and was proud of the products that the company produced.

While the boys continued their ball game, the girls gathered near the swing, taking turns swinging and playing with dolls that Izzie had made. Izzie not only made the dolls, but each doll had a complete wardrobe. Soon the dinner bell outside the back porch rang, and we gathered in what now seemed like an extremely small kitchen. As we stood around the kitchen table, heads bowed, listening to William say grace in Norwegian, I couldn't help but notice that each of the girls had a dress made of the same material I had modeled for Izzie. They were beautiful and even though hand made, looked store bought. These dresses made my own seem like a gunnysack.

When we finished the prayer, Izzie suggested that all the children "fill their plates" and eat at the tables outside. Izzie had two tables…one for the boys and one for the girls. The girls ate at the picnic table, and I suspected that the boys ate at the table that only yesterday had been the site of a bloody chicken massacre. Each table was covered with a red and white plaid tablecloth, complete with napkins and a centerpiece, which was a large pitcher of strawberry Kool-Aid.

Before I reached the table, Izzie touched my shoulder and said, "Julie, I need you to come into the sewing room for a second."

I followed Izzie into the sewing room, thinking that she might need me to help her with something. This room not only had Izzie's two Singers, but also a small writing desk and a chest-type freezer. Izzie pulled a box from between the freezer and the writing desk.

Izzie handed the box to me. "This is yours," she said. "I gave the other girls theirs earlier and just got yours finished this morning." I opened the box and immediately recognized the dress I had modeled a few days earlier. "Go ahead and put it on."

"But, Izzie I thought this dress was for Candace." I said as I quickly shed my other dress.

"I thought you probably did, Julie Belle. But you know I have been known to surprise people."

I smiled and thought of Izzie's gun. I also smiled (inside and out) when I walked out into the kitchen with my new dress on. The dress was such a special gift—made by such a special person.

As I sat with the other girls at the picnic table, eating our delicious fried chicken and scrumptious potato salad, I wondered if the other girls felt as I did about Izzie. I had no doubt that they did, but I was, perhaps, more fortunate. I could walk or ride my bike to Izzie's. All the others were miles away. I could enjoy Izzie's company nearly everyday in the summer.

The rest of the day was filled with ball playing, visiting, ice cream making, and the daily chores. The men piled all the boys in two cars and went to a real ball diamond in Lamont and three generations played America's favorite past time—baseball.

The women visited while washing an enormous pile of dishes. Visiting continued at the picnic table and later while preparing a late afternoon snack that would be eaten when the sweaty men and boys returned from the ball diamond.

I sat with the other girls on a blanket near one of the flower beds playing with some of Izzie's homemade dolls—dressing and undressing them. I secretly admired my dress and reflected on the past few days I'd spent with Izzie.

When the men and boys returned from Lamont, it was time to freeze ice cream. It was also time to bring the cows up to the barn for milking. Dad, Bill, and Ron volunteered to bring the cows up from the south pasture, while the other men and boys took turns cranking the ice cream maker. Ole' number nine roared through as my dad and brothers reached the railroad grade. Everyone in the yard stopped and waved at the train hoping it was engineered by Fred's brother George. On that day it was George! He waved and gave the whistle a few extra toots.

While the cows drank at the livestock tank and waited to be milked, we all ate once more— ham sandwiches, leftover potato salad, followed by pie and homemade vanilla ice cream. Everyone complimented Izzie on her cooking and told her how much fun the day had been.

As things wound down at the table, Fred announced that there were chores to do. This was his way of saying that now would be a good time to make an exit or be prepared to help with the chores. William and Gladys soon left to go play cards with friends for the evening. Jim, Dale, Larry, and their families went to Aurora for the evening festivities and to watch the fireworks. Aurora was known for its annual Fourth of July celebrations.

That left only my family at Fred and Izzie's. Dad and my brothers did the milking, while Fred continued to mow the hay field. I changed out of my new dress, checked for eggs, and fed the chickens for Izzie. Then I helped Izzie and Mom put things back in order around her house.

It wasn't long before the shadows from the tall pines covered the entire farmyard. Fred unhitched the horses from the mower and placed them in the barnyard just as Dad and my brothers let the cows out of the barn.

"Well, I didn't get the field finished. But they'll be another day," I heard Fred tell my dad. "How'd the milkin' go?

"Slow. I had to teach these rookies how to milk by hand," Dad said as he glanced at my brothers and chuckled.

Fred chuckled too.

Dad turned to my brothers, "Boys, herd Jerry and Ginger, and the cows to the south pasture and be sure to lock the gate behind them. I'll help with the hog chores, and we'll be done for the night."

We watched Aurora's fireworks from Izzie's picnic table. I drifted off to sleep snuggled between Izzie and Mom dreaming of my new dress, homemade ice cream, and fireworks.

Chapter 6 *Berry Picking*

It was a couple of days before I returned to Izzie's. I rode my bike and didn't arrive at Izzie's until after noon. Smokey barked a greeting and came running to me wagging his tail as I pulled the gate shut behind me. I guess he was anxious to see me. Izzie came out of the house carrying two pails.

"Julie Belle, are you ready to spend the rest of the day with me?" asked Izzie

"Sure, what are we going to do?" I questioned.

"Well, the black raspberries down along the railroad grade are ripe, and I'd like to pick enough for a couple of pies and a few batches of jam. Are you game for that?"

"Sure, but I might need a long-sleeved shirt. Aren't those bushes prickly?" I asked.

"I've got you covered, Julie Belle," Izzie answered.

Izzie was always prepared. She had an oversized shirt in one of the buckets. I think she must have been hoping I'd come by so we could go together. I surmised she didn't want to be alone, far from home, while picking the berries. There was a sense of security with two, and it would also make a hot, scratchy job a lot more fun.

Izzie wore her wide-brimmed hat and a lightweight jacket over her dress and apron. I assumed that since we were going to the railroad grade, she was carrying her pistol. As we walked down the cow lane toward the south pasture, we whistled and visited. I thanked Izzie again for the beautiful dress that she made me. She smiled, hugged me, and continued her whistling.

When we reached the railroad grade, Izzie and I turned east toward Lamont and waded through the knee deep grass until we reached the wild berry patch. There were black raspberries on both sides of the tracks, but those on the north side were better, according to Izzie. The hot summer sun didn't reach them and, as a result, they were bigger and juicier.

Izzie handed me my giant shirt and helped me roll up the sleeves just enough, so my hands peeked out from beneath the flannel. It was hot, and this shirt wasn't going to help me stay cool.

I soon forgot about the heat as we began the picking. Izzie was right. These were nice ripe berries, and I could pick three or four in a clump, which helped fill the pail faster. Izzie and I worked our way eastward through the berry patch chattering like two schoolgirls. It wasn't long and our pails were both about three-fourths full. Izzie and I both took a breather and wiped our brows on our sleeves. Our hands were scratched and our fingers were stained raspberry purple.

"Let's just pick for another half hour or so, and then we can herd the cows to the barn for tonight's milking," Izzie suggested. "Oh, and I have to do the milking tonight. Do you want to help me with that too?" Izzie asked.

"Sure, but what about Fred?" I questioned.

"Fred and your dad are going to bale some of the hay that he cut down. So, you won't have to ride your bike home tonight," Izzie informed me.

"How come no one told me?"

"I guess we talked about it after you fell asleep at the picnic table the other night."

Ole' number nine sounded its whistle in Aurora. Izzie and I picked as fast as we could to see how much we could pick before the train reached us. We made a game of it. We moved deeper into the ditch as the train drew near. Izzie commented that the berries looked picked over—like someone had already picked them. Our conversation was drowned as the locomotive and forty-seven cars barreled by. We waved at the engineer. Despite the deafening noise the breeze the train created felt good. My shirt and Izzie's light jacket were soaked with perspiration. We stood side by side mesmerized by the passing cars and felt the perspiration on our faces dry with each passing railroad car.

"Hello, ladies."

Startled at the male voice, Izzie and I both turned to face a scruffy stranger standing only a few yards to our left.

The man must have seen the fear and surprise on our faces. "I mean you no harm," the stranger assured us.

Izzie set her bucket down and casually placed her hand in her apron pocket. I felt a lot better knowing that Izzie was gripping the cold steel of her pistol.

"What's your business in this area?" Izzie asked rather callously.

"I'm just passing through, ma'am. I just picked some berries for my lunch and was napping when the train woke me. Good thing it did, or you might have stumbled right over me." The man's voice hesitated. His eyes dropped toward the ground and he scraped his foot in the grass. "Say, you don't know where a man could get a good home-cooked meal do you?"

"There's the Home Café about two miles ahead in Lamont. The meals are good there and reasonably priced," Izzie answered sternly.

The man raised his eyes briefly. "I have no money and have fallen on hard times. I couldn't pay for a meal."

"I'm afraid we can't help you. Good Luck," Izzie responded.

The stranger then turned away. "Thanks anyway, ma'am," he mumbled.

Izzie and I turned and headed back westward along the tracks, pails in hand, toward the south pasture gate. Suddenly, Izzie stopped, turned, and took a few steps back toward the man. By now he had his back turned and was walking away from us. Izzie hollered, "I'll leave some bread and boiled eggs by the gatepost when I turn the cows back into the south pasture tonight."

The man nodded and waved.

Izzie quickly rejoined me, and we walked briskly along the railroad tracks. I glanced back several times to make sure the stranger wasn't following us. We didn't speak until we reached the gate where the cows and horses were waiting. As Izzie reached for the gate, I could see her hand was shaking; I glanced up at her face and saw it was as white as chalk.

"Are you alright, Izzie?"

"Just feeling a little faint, Julie."

"I sure felt a lot better knowing you had your little pistol with you. I was…"

"I forgot the pistol," Izzie said, cutting me off. "I thought with the two of us and Smokey, we would be safe. Where is that damn dog anyway? Any other time he's lying under your feet."

Izzie rarely uttered a bad word, but I'm sure that even angels get frustrated now and then.

A series of sharp yelps answered Izzie's question. Smokey came bounding out of the creek bottom that ran through the south pasture chasing a rabbit for all he was worth. We watched as the rabbit leaped and zigzagged until it reached the safety of a woodpile.

"I guess he's a hunting dog not a guard dog," I said. Izzie smiled, and I noticed that the color had returned to her face.

"Looks like I'll be packing that man a lunch," Izzie sighed. "I'll also be packing the pistol from now on."

Izzie and I relaxed a bit as we followed the cows and horses toward the barnyard. But Izzie didn't whistle like she usually did. She just walked silently keeping her thoughts to herself.

Izzie and I were cooling off beneath the windmill when Fred arrived. He'd taken off work a little early, so he could rake the hay before Dad and my brothers got there to help with the baling. He parked the car in the shade and joined us. Izzie told him about the hobo we'd seen while picking berries. Fred scolded Izzie a little and reminded her why he'd given her the gun.

Fred looked at me and chuckled. "Julie, you look like you were in a fight with a wild cat."

"Nope, just some wild berry bushes," I replied.

Fred chuckled again and patted my head with his rugged right hand.

While Fred raked hay using the horsepower of Jerry and Ginger, Izzie and I did her chores as well as his. Before we started the milking, Izzie had me take the two pails of berries to the cellar. I returned with the milk strainer and a clean milk bucket.

Izzie was pretty handy with the milking. I giggled as she squirted the tomcat that sat in the aisle about six feet away. Izzie tried to squirt me too. But unlike the cat, I didn't want milk on me.

I was swinging on the bottom half of the barn door when the rest of my family pulled into Izzie's yard. It wasn't long before Dad had the John Deere hooked to the baler and the rickety hayrack. All three of my brothers bounced and balanced themselves on the wagon as they rumbled toward Fred. I gave Mom a quick hug when she arrived at the barn door. Izzie and I told her about the scruffy stranger we encountered while we were picking berries.

After the milking, we turned the cows out of the barn; I could see Bill leading Jerry and Ginger toward the barnyard. Izzie suggested that Bill and I herd the cows and the work horses to the south pasture for the night. As I started out the barn door to meet Bill, Izzie placed her hand on my shoulder and took me aside. By now, Mom was in the house setting the table for Izzie.

"Julie Belle, I need you to run to the house, get the paper bag on the porch, and place it by the gatepost," Izzie whispered and then winked at me. "Keep this under your hat. I'm sure Fred wouldn't approve of me giving that stranger food."

I nodded and took off for the house.

I kept the bag under my shirt while Bill and I herded the livestock to the south pasture; I told him about the encounter with the hobo. We both wondered how terrible it must be to not know where you were going to get your next meal or where you were going to sleep every night. We finally decided that it might be as scary for a hobo as it was for those of us who were scared of them. While Bill herded the horses and cows over the railroad grade, I was able to place the bag beside the gatepost as Izzie had instructed.

As we walked back from the south pasture, Bill jumped the fence and cut across the hayfield to the tractor and baler. I could hear a lot of hollering, and Fred sputtering a few obscenities about the new-fangled baler. There was a lot of stopping and starting, and the stack of bales on the wagon wasn't growing very quickly. From what I'd gathered from Izzie, Fred wasn't embracing the changes that were occurring in agriculture. He wouldn't think of spending money on brand new equipment. He settled for used equipment that was new to him. But, what was *new* to him, most likely had been someone else's *old* headache. From the sound of it, this was definitely the case with the baler.

It was dark before the guys came in from the field with a load of hay. Fortunately, the man on the radio said there was no rain in the forecast. That was good because the haymaking didn't go very well. After a quick supper, Izzie chased us out the door and back to town with the agreement that we could come back tomorrow evening for more haymaking and a slice of black raspberry pie. Everyone left excited about the pie, but I wasn't sure about the haymaking.

Chapter 7

Taking the Tracks

My family went to Izzie's nearly every night that week and helped with the haymaking. The knotter on the baler that mechanically ties each twine string, worked so poorly that Dad had to ride on the back of the baler and tie each knot by hand. This was a typical example of Fred's struggle with change. Fred's struggle could be described as a battle of horse and man versus tractor and machinery. Izzie's struggle was similar, but I began to realize that it was more of a battle between her desire for change and Fred's resistance to change. But Izzie was loyal to Fred, as women were in those days, and accepting what life sent her way was the norm. And, of course, Izzie whistled and found a way to make the most of it.

It rained for several days after the hay was made. The creeks and rivers ran either right to the tops of their banks or flooded. When the weather broke, I was anxious to get back to Izzie's. I thought about the creek I had to cross on the Lockwood farm. It could be waist deep with all the rain we'd had. Then I realized that I had left my bike at Izzie's during the haymaking and would have to walk along the railway. I thought about the railroad dangers that Mom and Izzie had often warned me about. There was a risk that ole' number nine might pass through or that I might be confronted by a hobo. I decided to take my chances. Even though I hadn't taken the railroad tracks by myself before, I had walked it once with my brothers. At least it would be dry.

From home, I walked through downtown and hopped on the tracks near the grain elevator. The tracks took me by numerous coal and grain bins, behind the schoolyard, and past the bus barn where Mr. Dozark was working on a bus. I passed the feed mill at the very west side of town and was now in the country.

When I wasn't gawking at the scenery, it was fun to see how far I could walk on the rails without falling off. With a little practice, I became pretty good at it. As I walked along, I noticed how wild and grown up some of the areas were between town and Izzie's place. There was wildlife galore. Birds chattered all around me. Meadow larks, red-winged blackbirds, bobolinks, and several species of sparrows surrounded me and filled the air with their songs. Pheasants cackled as the day warmed. Ahead of me a red fox paused briefly on the tracks to watch my balancing act.

It wasn't long before I could see Izzie's farm and also the railroad bridge that stretched across the swollen creek. The railroad bridge wasn't very high or very long, but I remembered, when I was with my brothers, not liking that the spaces between the railroad ties allowed you to see to the creek below. I envisioned getting my foot or leg wedged between the ties and being stuck on the bridge as a train approached. I shook my head to get that thought out of my mind. It was too nice a day for that kind of thinking, and I was actually getting pretty good at balancing on the rails as I walked. I thought of the circus and imagined being a tightrope walker until I reached the edge of the bridge.

I stopped when I reached the bridge. I peered down between the railroad ties and watched the swift, swirling water beneath. I took a deep breath and pretended that I was under the *big top* about to cross the high wire above thousands of circus fans. I took a bow and placed my feet on the shiny rail. My soiled canvas shoes weren't exactly what I had pictured, but they would carry me swiftly and safely to the other side. I walked with my arms stretched out, teetering this way and that. The noise from the swollen creek sounded a little like the distant chattering and sighing of the circus crowd. I was nearly across the bridge, with only a step or two to go. I imagined the crowd cheering as I was about to step to the safety of the other side.

Out of the corner of my eye, I caught a glimpse of something moving near the rail by my feet. A large snake lay coiled, apparently sunning himself, within inches of my right foot. I instinctively jumped to my left toward the other side of the tracks. One of my shoelaces caught in a joint where two rails were joined together. The extraordinary balance I had just exhibited while crossing the bridge was gone. I twisted my body, so I would fall away from the snake. As I was falling, I heard my left ankle crack, and then my right temple smacked the rail on the other side. I felt a sharp pain in my head and then a buzz, almost like I'd gotten an electrical shock. Everything went black.

While I lay there unconscious, I floated from the circus tent, to Izzie's, and then home. It was all good but really mixed up. It was like I was sleeping but couldn't wake up. I tried to will myself into consciousness but just couldn't get past the black barrier. In the distance a train blew its whistle and blew its whistle again. The whistle grew louder and blew numerous times. Izzie had told me you could always tell when there was livestock on the tracks by the way the whistle blew. Maybe the Gates' cows were on the tracks. I wondered.

The train blew its whistle again, again, and again. It was deafening. The ground shook all around me. I could hear the squealing of steel wheels on steel tracks like I'd never heard them before. Suddenly I felt someone lift me. I felt my left shoe pulled from my foot. The train blew its whistle yet again. My head throbbed, buzzed, and things went very black.

I awoke with someone holding me close and wiping a damp cool cloth across my face. When my eyes focused, I could see it was Izzie. I struggled to see where I was. I was in Izzie's yard, lying on the stone boat beneath the shady white pines. The scruffy man Izzie and I had seen by the tracks was holding Jerry and Ginger by the reins.

"What happened, Izzie?" I whispered.

Izzie shushed me. "I'll tell you all about it later. Let's just say that angels don't always wear white."

Just then, a car pulled into Izzie's drive. Doc Ford and his nurse, Marge, came to my side. Doc gave me a brief examination. I heard him tell Izzie that my ankle was definitely broken, but he was more concerned about my head. Marge held a white cloth and an ice bag over the wound on my head.

I looked down at my feet, as I lay there. I had one shoe on and one shoe off, and blood was spattered on my clothes. I thought of Wally and the chicken butchering, and things went black again.

Chapter 8 *Recovery*

I was surrounded by white when I resurfaced again. White walls, white curtains, white sheets, white gowns, and an extremely bright light shining on me. Two smiling, angel-like, faces smiled down on me— Izzie's and Mom's.

"Are we in heaven?" I asked groggily.

"No, Julie you're at Mercy Hospital in Oelwein," Mom answered and then began to cry.

"How did I get here?"

"Doc Ford and Nurse Marge brought you," Izzie explained.

"How come I don't remember it?

"You were unconscious," Mom said, her voice cracking. "The blow you took to your head was pretty serious." A tear fell from her cheek to the white sheet on the bed, and Izzie wiped her eyes with her neatly ironed handkerchief. Mom and Izzie each leaned over the rail of my bed and gingerly hugged me and kissed me on the only part of my forehead that wasn't covered by bandages.

Mom and Izzie didn't stay in my room long enough for me to get any details from them. A nurse came in, chased them back to the waiting area, and lowered the shade that was letting the bright July sunshine into my room. She gave me a drink of ice water and instructed me to rest.

Resting wasn't a problem in the hospital. I had a headache most of the time and my leg was encased in plaster all the way to my knee. I thought a lot about my accident. There were a lot of questions that I needed to ask Mom and Izzie when I got home. I wanted to know who moved me from the tracks. Why was the scruffy man holding Jerry and Ginger by the reins? How did Doc Ford and Marge happen on the scene? And finally, what did Izzie mean when she said that angels don't always wear white? I guessed the answers to these questions would just have to wait until I got home. It seemed that all Izzie and Mom had to give were tears, hugs, and kisses.

My stay in the hospital wasn't too long—only four days or so. Mom, Dad, Fred, and Izzie visited me when the nurses would let them. I also received a nice *Get Well* card from Nancy. I left there anxious to get back home, healed up, and, of course, back to Izzie's. A severe concussion, a few stitches, and a broken leg weren't going to spoil the rest of my summer.

Chapter 9 *The Real Story*

My injuries had been worse than I thought. Even after going home, I was restricted to bed rest and minimal physical activity for about two weeks. My headaches gradually subsided, and Doc Ford eventually took the twelve stitches out of my scalp. I mastered my crutches in a relatively short time. I had to. My brothers waited on me and treated me like a queen for the first week, but soon baseball and other activities lured them out of the house more and more. Mom took time off from her summer classes and did her schoolwork at home while nursing me back to health.

I gradually got the details of the accident from Mom during our time together. Apparently the train was only a few feet away when I was lifted off the tracks. The scruffy man Izzie and I had seen while picking berries had set up camp beneath the railroad bridge. He had watched me balance my way across the bridge but didn't realize I had fallen until the train kept blowing its whistle. When he made his way up the grade from beneath the bridge, the train was only seconds away from striking me. He scooped me up and out of the way just as the train screeched by. The train had actually set its brakes to stop, which was why the noise was so intense.

The train never came to a complete stop. The engine was several hundred yards beyond the bridge toward Lamont as the caboose rolled slowly by. The conductor came out of the caboose, and the scruffy man told him to send back help when they reached Lamont. The conductor signaled ahead to the engineer, who luckily was George, and the train crept into Lamont, where the conductor contacted Doc Ford. George told him whose farm to send him to.

Izzie had heard the train's distress signal. She knew there was trouble and was watching the activity from the barn door. The scruffy man waved his arms at Izzie. Izzie could see someone lying along the grade, and she was afraid it was me. She ran into the house and got some warm water from the teakettle and some clean dish towels. She ran them to the stone boat, which was the only thing she had suitable to pull someone along and out of the railroad ditch. It took some time to hitch the horses to it, but soon Izzie and the makeshift transport arrived at my side. Izzie and I rode on the stone boat, my head cradled in her arms, as the scruffy man drove the horses through the ditch and the berry bushes to the yard. According to Izzie, it was only a few minutes after we reached the yard that Doc and Nurse Marge arrived.

Izzie rode with us to Mercy Hospital in Oelwein. I guess Doc made it in about fifteen minutes, which meant he made a lot of dust fly. Once in the hospital, Doc stitched my head and another doctor set my leg and put it in a cast. Doc had left patients sitting in the waiting room, so as soon as he felt I was stable, he and Marge returned to his office. Izzie stayed and prayed.

When Fred came home for the evening, he found the scruffy man doing what chores he could. He told Fred about the accident and that Izzie was at the hospital. Fred realized that my parents might not know about the accident, so he drove to Lamont to tell my family. He also realized that a telephone would have certainly saved a lot of time and perhaps even a life. When he arrived at our home, Mom and Dad were just backing out our driveway to leave for the hospital. They learned about the accident from Marge after she and Doc returned from Oelwein.

Fred took my brothers back to the farm with him. Fred, the scruffy man, and my brothers got the evening chores done in short order. When the chores were done, the men and boys ate some of Izzie's leftovers, and Fred drove the scruffy man into Lamont to spend the night at the hotel. He paid for two nights lodging and gave the man enough money to buy some meals and new clothes. He also found out that the man's name was Ben and that he was a WWII veteran from Kansas who had lost his family in a house fire while he was overseas.

Things didn't return to *near* normal for anyone until the day I awoke and saw Izzie and Mom at my bedside. I guess I had actually lapsed in and out of consciousness for a couple of days.

Chapter 10 *Changes*

    In August, Mom drove me to Izzie's to spend my last two weeks of summer vacation. Things had changed since my accident. One of Izzie's wishes came true—she got her telephone installed. While I was still in the hospital Fred contacted the telephone company, and the phone was installed one day while Izzie was visiting me. From then on, Izzie and Mom kept close track of my whereabouts and the whereabouts of a few others as well.

    During my stay at Izzie's, we canned green beans and tomatoes, froze sweet corn, and picked the blackberries that grew in the fence row between the Gaffney farm and Izzie's. We, actually mostly Izzie, painted the chicken house, the woodshed, and the south side of the corncrib. Despite my broken leg and crutches, I contributed as much help as I could.

Nearly every weekend the rest of that summer and autumn, my family came out to the farm to help with something. Dad and Fred repaired the gearbox on the windmill and also the knotter on the baler. The second cutting of hay went better than the first. We all enjoyed many of Izzie's meals. Even Ben, who now didn't look so scruffy, came one Sunday for dinner. He took a job with Mr. Prindle, one of the carpenters in town, and planned to stay in Lamont for awhile.

My cast came off shortly after school started. It was good to be able to walk, run, ride a bike, and scratch my leg without the aid of a ruler. Once school began my visits to Izzie's were limited to weekends. But now, my entire family was involved with most of the activities on Izzie's farm. We all helped get Izzie and Fred ready for winter. The men picked the corn crop and butchered a hog while Izzie, Mom, and I harvested and put up the produce from Izzie's garden. In return, we got lots of wonderful home-cooked meals, a lot of family time, and lots of fruit, vegetables, and meat for the winter. And, of course, many of Izzie's whistle serenades. By the first snowfall, Izzie and Fred, and our family were prepared for the long Iowa winter.

That summer at Izzie's was a time to reflect on how the new replaced the old—tractors replaced horses and machines replaced the manual labor done by men and women on the farm. Times had already changed for the farms that surrounded Izzie's and change was inevitable for both Izzie and Fred, too. With change, wishes and dreams would come true, but hearts would also be broken. My accident and the installation of the telephone seemed to be a tipping point for both Fred and Izzie. Machines and household gadgets were becoming the way of the world, and over the course of the next few years many changes occurred.

Fred retired the following summer, and sold the cows and the horses. It was a sad day when Mr. Miller drove his truck away from Izzie's carrying the six Jersey cows to the Nelson farm a few miles away. Many tears were shed when Jerry and Ginger made their last trip down the driveway led by a couple of Amish men from Hazelton. Fred kept his hogs, and Izzie kept her chickens. They made changes gradually.

Fred eventually replaced nearly all of his horse-drawn machinery with implements that could be pulled by the tractor. He admitted that it made his life easier. It was a lot easier and faster to harvest the corn crop with a machine rather than by hand. He was still about fifteen to twenty years behind the neighbors, though.

As for Izzie, she gradually received many of her wishes—running water (both hot and cold), a new kitchen sink and faucet, a new bathroom with a stool and tub, and a laundry room with an automatic washer and dryer. Izzie was beside herself for a while. No more trips to the outhouse or to the windmill for water, and she no longer had to heat water for dishes or laundry. Just turn on the faucet, and there it was. Of course, these changes didn't eliminate most of Izzie's work; they just made it easier. In time she got a gas-powered lawnmower and a TV (which Fred took control of); Izzie even learned to drive a car at the *young* age of seventy.

That summer at Izzie's, when I was eleven-years-old, is a memory I will always treasure. It was a time of change for me, too. My life was changed forever. By the end of the summer, I didn't need to ask what Izzie meant when she said, "Angels don't always wear white." Many angels touched me that summer—several were sent to me to save my life that fateful day on the train tracks. They lifted me, transported me, and hovered around me as I lay helpless and unconscious. Rarely did any of them wear white, but *one* did whistle. That **one** was also my grandmother!

Made in the USA
Charleston, SC
19 April 2011